M   g!

Please return/renew this item by the last
date shown. Books may also be renewed
by phone or Internet.

 www.rbwm.gov.uk/web/libraries.htm

☎   01628 796969 (library hours)

☎   0303 123 0035 (24 hours)

The Royal Borough
Windsor &
Maidenhead

To Tom, Sarah,
Nigel, Sabrina and Kim
for their kind help
and advice

Mummy Laid an Egg!
by
Babette Cole

Red Fox

"Right," said mum and dad.
"We think it's time we
   told you

how babies are made."

"OK," we said.

"Girl babies are made from sugar and spice
and all things nice," said mum.

"Boy babies are made from slugs and snails and puppy dogs' tails," said dad.

"Some babies are delivered by dinosaurs."

"You can make them out of gingerbread," said mum.

"Sometimes you just find them under stones," said dad.

"You can grow them from seeds in pots

" n the greenhouse," said mum.

"Or just squidge them out
   of tubes."

"Mummy laid an egg on the sofa," said dad.
"It ...

... exploded.

And you shot out."

"Hee hee hee, ha ha ha, hoo hoo hoo. What a load of rubbish," we laughed.
"But you were nearly right about the SEEDS, the TUBE and the EGG."

"We don't think you know how babies are really made. So we're doing some drawings to show you."

"Mummy does have eggs. They are inside her tummy."

"And daddy has seeds in seed pods outside his body."

This fits

"Daddy also has a tube. The seeds from the pods come out of it."

in here

"The tube goes into
mummy's tummy through
a little hole. Then the seeds
swim inside using their tails."

"Here are some ways

mummies and daddies
fit together."

"The baby gets bigger

Mummy gets fatter

"So now YOU know…

...and so does everyone else!"

A Red Fox Book

Published by Random House Children's Books
20 Vauxhall Bridge Road, London SW1V 2SA

A division of Random House UK Ltd
London Melbourne Sydney Auckland
Johannesburg and agencies throughout the world

Copyright © Babette Cole 1993

10

First published in Great Britain by Jonathan Cape Ltd 1993

Red Fox edition 1995

Printed and bound in Hong Kong

RANDOM HOUSE UK Limited Reg. No. 954009

ISBN 0 09 929911 9

Some
bestselling Red Fox
picture books